For Stefan

Table of contends

The caller

Hanna stood at the window with a cup of coffee in her hand, looked out and noticed that the sun was shining. She has been sleeping a little better for two weeks now.
Fortunately, the antidepressants prescribed by Dr. Klein finally seemed to work after three weeks, but unfortunately, they did not help against her nightmares. She still woke up night after night in a sweat and her heart was beating up to her neck. The doctor thought it was a perfectly normal reaction after such a severe trauma as the one she had experienced. She just had to be patient enough with herself; the doctor advised her that eventually, everything

would be okay again. However, she remained sceptical because half a year had passed since David had died.

She closed her eyes to live through it again how the car started to roll, went off the road and crashed into a tree. David lay dead beside her; a thick branch had pierced him. Her limbs, however, were grotesquely twisting in all directions, and she had a heavily bleeding laceration on her forehead.
As she opened her eyes again, she swayed. Hanna, therefore, had to lean on the kitchen table for a few seconds; otherwise, she would have fallen over.
According to the police report, David had simply driven too fast. Nevertheless, Hanna knew

4

that this was not true because just before David lost control of the car, another vehicle was waiting for them.

The driver of the other vehicle had forced their car off the road and then committed a hit and run.

She tore herself away from the agonizing thoughts then looked at the watch. At 7.30 a.m., it was time to get ready for her session with Dr. Klein.

While she was about to go into the bedroom to get dressed, the phone rang unexpectedly.

When she picked up the receiver, a deep male voice answered, "We should talk to each other," the stranger explained.

"I know who killed your boyfriend."

"We are meeting this afternoon at 15 o'clock in the City Park. Please come alone."

Hanna was about to ask whom she was talking to, how he knew her and how he knew about the accident, but at that very moment the stranger ended the phone call, she only heard the endless ringing of the dial tone.
For a moment, she wondered if this call was just a figment of her imagination. Since the accident, she could not always trust her perception. "Maybe it's a consequence of the brain injury," she suspected. "It's quite possible that I'm not quite well yet," thought Hanna so, she dressed.

Tom Klein sat in his office at 7:45 a.m., as he did every

morning, to prepare for his first patient. She was suffering from post-traumatic stress disorder. For half a year, he had not been able to get any significant Progress.

He was putting the book on traumatology back on the shelf to his right when his secretary came in to bring him an extra-strong cup of coffee.

"Good morning, doctor!"
"Morning, Glenda. Please send in the patient."
"Will do," replied the secretary and left the room.

Hanna entered the treatment room and took a seat in the brown armchair next to the window. Nervously she wiped a blonde curl out of her forehead with her left hand.

"How are you?" The doctor asked he fixed her through his thick glasses.

"How are the nightmares?"

"They are still the same."

"Did you write down the contents of your dream after you woke up, as I recommended?"

"Yes, but I don't see any use for me."

"The point of this is to understand your dreams better and learn how to control them."

"Psychology also refers to this as lucid dreaming."

"Okay, I just doubt it works that way."

"Practice makes perfect."

"In time. Success is already set."

"Is there anything else you want to discuss with me today?"

"No," she replied. She did not intend to tell him about the

call; it was not important
anyway.

"All right," said Dr. Klein.
"The medications are taking you
well enough?"

"Except for the dry mouth, I
can't complain."

"Wonderful, I'll see you next
week," he said.

Finally, the doctor shook her
hand as a farewell gesture.
After the session, Hanna
decided to stroll through the
city. She looked into the
window displays, a green blouse
she liked especially well, but
she did not have enough money
with her, so she had to do
without. She also wanted to lie
on the comfortable couch in her
living room as soon as
possible, because this was one
of her favourite places at the
time.

When she finally arrived home, she put the key in the lock, opened the door and got scared - the apartment resembled a battlefield. All drawers been torn out, and whoever had entered the apartment had ruthlessly spread her things all over the floor. Silently, Hanna pulled a can of pepper spray from her coat pocket and entered the apartment in fear. After making sure that no one else was there, she rushed to the phone to call the police. The police officer a quarter-hour later arrived at her apartment and was standing in the door; he seemed two meters tall. He had a frightening aura that intimidated her a bit. Beneath his uniform, a muscular body stood out, which Hanna found quite sexy.

"Well, you called us about a burglary?" asked the officer. At the same time, he checked the door for signs of a break-in. He recognised immediately that it was unscathed.

"Yes, I did."

"What is your name?"

"Hanna Mooreland."

"Has anything been stolen?"

"No, I don't think so."

"All right."

"But this morning I got a strange phone call. A man called to say he knew who was responsible for the accident that killed my fiancé. At first, I didn't think anything of it, but now I wonder if there could be a connection."

"Really?" The officer replied and looked around the room with interest.

Besides all the mess the burglar had left behind, he noticed several empty wine bottles and a can of psychotropic drugs. For him, it was a clear case of too much alcohol in combination with medication. For a moment, he thought about whether he should tell her his suspicion.

Then he said, "Miss Mooreland, I think everything seems to be in perfect order here. You have nothing further to worry about."
"But what about the caller?"
"Well, I guess it was just a bad joke."
"Maybe the joker has read about the accident in the newspaper."
"Are you sure?"
"There are some weirdos that get a kick out of it."

"Don't worry your pretty little head about it; it's a waste of time." With these words, the giant said goodbye.

Hanna did not want to share his opinion. Too many things just did not fit together. She decided to call Brenda because she could always rely on her opinion. Her sister often looked at things from a different perspective, which helped her to see new aspects.

Brenda Turkins was standing in the cellar to put the laundry in the dryer, when the phone rang. She pulled the phone out of the trouser pocket, answering "Hello Han ..." That was all she could get because Hanna fell into her word.

She sounded very excited, which since her accident caused her to start stuttering.

"C-Can you come tonight?"
"Sure, but what's wrong with you?"
"I've been burgled! I just don't want to be alone tonight."
"Oh God, that's terrible!"
"Did you call the police?"
"Y-yes, I did, but I didn't feel like I was being s-special taken seriously. Idiots!"
"Okay, I'll be there tonight around 7:30!"
"I'll see you soon."
"Thanks" Hanna replied reassured.

Then Brenda went to the kitchen, put a kettle of water on and brewed herself a tea. "Poor thing" she thought, "she's been through so much already."

After Brenda's visit, Hanna sat in her living room, the TV running alongside. She was feeling a little better now. It had obviously done her good that her sister had come; the two of them had been inseparable since childhood. Whenever she felt bad, her big sister was the rock in the surf. Hanna reviewed the day once again. The police officer and Brenda were certainly right, and the phone call was just a nasty prank. After all, there were more than enough idiots running around today who took a liking to something like that. After half an hour, she felt her eyelids become heavy, and she sank into a deep sleep. When she was asleep, however,

she did not notice how quietly
the room door opened.
Someone came close to her and
hissed, "We're going to finish
you off," and then the stranger
sneaked away quietly.

A few weeks had already passed
since Hanna had received this
mysterious call, and the break-
in was already forgotten.
"Fortunately" she thought,
"things were looking up again."
After all this hard time, at
least a light shone at the end.
That is why she wanted to
meet her best friend she had
not seen for a long time again.
A little entertainment was not
a bad idea after all.

As she entered the restaurant,
Lilly was already there sipping
her iced coffee, her reddish-
brown braided hair shining

golden in the sun. Hanna sat down across from her, and her best friend immediately started to eye her urgently.

"You look good," Lilly said firmly.
"Thanks for the compliment."
After a few minutes, a stocky waitress came to her table and asked Hanna "What can I get you?"

"A turkey breast salad with a sugar-free iced tea please," she replied.
"Coming right up."
"What's it like for you to go back to work?" Lilly started the conversation curiously.
"Pretty good. Sometimes, I still feel overwhelmed, but I am glad that the nightmares have subsided."
"I believe you."

"How are you?" Hanna asked.
"I am fine.
A month ago, I started a new job at the newspaper in the city."
"Oh, that's great!"
"Yeah, I've been looking for a long time, until I found the right job."
Meanwhile, the waitress came back panting with the salad; you could clearly see that she was an old woman.
"Enjoy it; it looks really good; maybe I'll have one of those."
"Why not!" Hanna agreed.
Then she took a big bite and let the creamy sweet and sour taste dance on her tongue.

After they finished eating, Hanna walked back to her car. A paper was stuck on the windshield wiper.

"Shit, not another parking ticket!" She murmured unnervingly.

However, when she read it, her knees threatened to go soft "Why didn't you come?" was writing on it in handwritten letters. She hastily put the note in her handbag. Her hands trembled like aspen leaves; she barely managed to open the car door, fell on to the seat and started the engine. She stepped on the gas pedal with all her might and hardly noticed that she almost collided with a bus.

"Yes, yes, I'm coming" called Brenda and laboriously rose from the rocking chair in which she was dozing off just now. She shuffled to the door, looked through the peephole, pushed the handle down and saw a completely disintegrated Hanna.

She stammered, "S-somebody stuck this piece of paper on my windshield wiper" c-clamped.

Excitedly she rummaged through her bag, but no matter how hard she searched, the piece of paper was simply not to be found. "T-that can't be!"

"What is it?"

"The note was s-still here a-and now it's gone."

Brenda looked at Hanna with her green eyes, worried.

"Could it be that she hasn't recovered yet?" She asked herself.

In the first months after the accident, Hanna had often been confused. Moreover, she had been struggling with considerable memory problems at that time. It was only thanks to her good friend Lilly that she found a doctor who was willing to take on all these problems.

"Sit down; I'll make us some tea. And then we can have a nice, chat."

Hanna sat down on the purple couch. She looked around and realised that Brenda still hadn't unpacked all moving boxes. Her sister had been living here for a month since she had separated from her husband. Brenda came back with a tray on which a porcelain pot and two cups stood. She took one of the coasters to put it on the table, slowly put the tray down and poured the tea.

"So" she began, "tell me, what happened?"

"I had dinner with L-Lilly today; we went to the Grill

House. Afterwards, as I was walking to my car, there was a n-note on the windshield wiper with the message that he was waiting for me."

"Who was waiting for you?" Brenda had a sip of tea.

"The guy who called me. I put the note in my pocket to show it to you, and now it is suddenly disappeared", she explained excitedly.

"But how could you lose it when you hat it plugged in?"

"I don't know. Maybe it was removed from the bag, when I put the bag down for a moment in the parking garage."

"Okay, could be. Are you really sure that you didn't just imagine this."

"Yes, a-am I" sighed Hanna resignedly.

"Well" said Brenda, knowing it was pointless anyway to convince her sister from the opposite.

Right after Hanna left, she carried the dishes into the kitchen. The story seemed very strange to her. "Maybe I should keep a closer eye on her," Brenda considered. She was very worried about the whole thing.

Meanwhile, Lilly was lying in bed next to him. She didn't get a wink, stared at the ceiling and listened to his snoring. Not that it bothered her much, no, that wasn't the reason she couldn't find sleep. "Is it really right what we do?" "If it gets out, we will be behind bars for years," she feared. He, on the other hand, was convinced that everything would go fine. "Why should anything go wrong?"

"Once it's gone, we'll be free" he believed. "Why did Hanna and David have to be there that very night? If only she hadn't argued with him..."

"Stop, you have to stop brooding!"

"There's no point, it can't be helped anyway,"
she whispered into the darkness.

She got up to go to the bathroom. Lilly splashed cold water on her face to cool down; then she went back to bed. She could tell from his breathing that he was no longer in a deep sleep.

She laid her head on his shoulder "I can't sleep."

"Why?" He yawned extensively.

"You know why, because of what happened."

"We've seen this for thousands of years.
Chewed through times." He looked at her irritated.
Lilly's face reddened within seconds.
"I don't care!" She almost shouted. "If something goes wrong, we're both in deep shit!" Hot tears were streaming down her cheeks.
Now his gaze became softer. With a soothing voice, he continued to say, "Don't worry! I've got everything under control. One of these days, that chick is going to crack. Then she'll either end up in a psychiatric ward or take her own life, whichever occurs first," and
smiled maliciously.
"Your word in God's ear," she replied.

"I only hope you're right because I'd rather not see what happens if it goes wrong."
"Now, don't worry so much, everything will be all right" he pressed her firmly to confirm this.
It almost seemed as if he was trying to remove all her doubts with this gesture.

Some more yellow. "Yes, it looks great" Brenda thought. The painting was almost finished; the next vernissage would certainly be a success. She just had to manage to get out of the red.
"This year will certainly be better," she said loudly to herself.
In a moment, she expected her next client Dr. Klein. It was somewhat strange to portray her sister's doctor, but why not?

He planned to hang the picture
in the waiting room of his
office.
The bell rang, "Right on time,"
she thought.

"Did you get through the
traffic well?" She asked her
guest and took off his coat.
"Of course, as always when I
come to you" the doctor put on
a charming smile.
"You charmer!"
"Please take a seat on the
bench and hold the position."
She took the brush and the
palette back into her
hand.
"Will do."
He sat down with his upper body
turned slightly to the right,
certainly not a pleasant
posture.
Brenda noticed that he seemed
very loose, so very different

from the way Hanna described him. She dipped the brush into the paint and began to paint. While she worked,
she considered talking to him about Hanna for a moment. Of course, it was clear that he was subject to confidentiality, but she simply thought about it.

"I would like to take the opportunity to discuss something with you," she began the conversation.
"I am all ears; what is it about?"
"It's about my sister."
"You know I'm bound by doctor-patient confidentiality."
"I know" she replied, embarrassed, "but I am afraid that Hanna is gradually losing her sense of reality."

The physician became attentive. "What exactly do you mean by this?"

"My sister feels persecuted."

"She is convinced someone is after her, someone involved in the accident."

"I am astonished to hear this."

"I never before had the impression that she was delusionally paranoid."

"I didn't claim that she was delusional," explained Brenda him.

A soft splashing could be heard from outside. It had started to rain, and a relaxed atmosphere filled the room.

"I see."

"I could speak to your sister about this at your next appointment if you'd like."

"That would make me feel very calm."

"But" Brenda replied hastily, "Under no circumstances tell her I spoke to you!"

"No."

"Don't worry about that."

"Thank you," replied Brenda with audible relief.

The trap is set!

Tick tock tick tock! Even an inconspicuous sound like the ticking of the clock was enough to get on Hanna's nerves. Every minute she thought of the phone ringing again and then this guy.

A few weeks ago, she thought it was just a harmless prank phone call, but now she had the impression of being caught in a nightmare again, only that this time it was in reality.

In the beginning, the calls
could be ignored without any
problems.
However, after a while, the
friendly tone of the stalker
changed and violent insults
such as "You bitch!" or "I'm
going to kill you!" had become
the order of the day...
However, the bitter thing for
her was that Brenda no longer
believed her. She never said it
directly, but her behaviour
said it all. Every time she
rolled her eyes, every time
Hanna wanted to talk to her
about it, it stung her heart a
little. To make matters worse,
Lilly had begun to withdraw
from her more and more, which
made her very sad.
The scumbag who was chasing her
usually liked to leave his
messages on the windshield
wiper, but also in the mailbox

or at the apartment door. She would have liked to show the messages to Brenda, but it was like being bewitched whenever she intended to do so, the notes were swallowed like from the ground. It was, in the truest sense of the word, maddening. "Well, no matter what," she thought, "anyway, today I have to go to this psychiatrist again, and it's time to get going; otherwise I'll be late."

On the way to her appointment, a man sat in front of her on the bus, who kept looking at her with a penetrating look. Under other circumstances, she would not have thought about it, but now she automatically asked herself if he was the one who had been stalking her for weeks. When the bus stopped,

and she was able to get off,
she clearly felt a weight fall
from her shoulders.
Arriving at her destination,
Hanna stepped into the waiting
room and sat down on one of the
very comfortable chairs.
Meanwhile, the secretary
continued to tap stoically on
her typewriter. She found it
strange that someone still used
a typewriter to this day.
Apparently, Dr. Klein had a
sense for nostalgia. The whole
office was furnished in this
style, which she liked very
much from the first minute. It
simply radiated a certain
calmness. After a quarter of an
hour, the secretary told her
that she could now come into
the consulting room.

She returned to the brown

armchair seat. Dr. Klein looked
at her briefly while he noted
something else in the file.

Finally, as always, he began
with the most important
question.
"How are you doing today?"
Hanna thought about what to
answer, then she said, "I'm
fine."
"Really?"
He followed up and looked over
at her with a sceptical
authoritarian expression on his
face.
She looked at the floor and
felt caught.
"Yes, you're right" she
gathered all her courage.
"I-I've been p-persecuted for
weeks," she confessed."
"I haven't talked to you t-till
now because I m-mean that you

can't help me with this problem anyway."

"Well, maybe you could just let me give it a try" he leaned back comfortably into his boss chair.

"Why don't you tell me what happened?"

"Well, I don't really know where to start."

"It's been about eight weeks since I received a call from a stranger in the morning. He told me that he knew the person who caused the accident and would like to meet me. Of course, I was completely perplexed" she faltered. Then she continued.

"But before I could ask him who it was, the guy hung up on me", she drank two sips of water. Her throat felt like sandpaper "But", she paused again, "that's n-not all. When I came

home that day I found my
apartment completely
ransacked."
"All sounds very bad" he said
compassionately.
"Yes, as I already mentioned at
the beginning, I am being
stalked s-side with phone calls
and written messages."
"In the beginning, w-was all
quite harmless, but in the
meantime, it has become pure
horror!"
Hanna collapsed like a
pile of misery.
"It's understandable that you
feel this way. Have you already
informed the police?"
"Of course! Only the p-police
told me they couldn't do
anything."
"Is there anything I can do for
you? "
"Nice of you to ask, but I
don't see what you can do."

"How do you sleep?"
"Badly, according to circumstances."
"In that case, I suggest we try Zopiclone."

Dr. Klein pulled out his prescription pad. Hanna was not very enthusiastic about it, because psycho pills were nothing more than drugs for her. After her last experience, she could do without them.

"Take a tablet before going to bed," he told and gave her the prescription.
She finally accepted it with great reluctance.

When his last patient left the office that day, Tom put on his coat and went into the outer office to say goodbye to Glenda. "See you tomorrow," he said as he passed by, and then he disappeared with quick steps out the door.

Down the street, a woman was waiting for him, holding a purple umbrella in her left hand.

Tom looked at Lilly in amazement, and then asked happily, "Why are you here?"

"I've been shopping, and since your office was on the way, I thought I'd stop by to check on you," she put her arms on his shoulders. He returned the hug tenderly.

"How's our plan going?" Lilly wanted to know.

"I can't complain we are making progress only it should slowly move into phase two."

"So now it's my turn."

"Exactly," he replied.

"Okay, but I don't have a good

feeling on the matter."

"I can understand that," he said, looking at her with understanding.

"However, we have no other choice, so be a good girl!"

He gave her a light slap on the butt, Lilly giggled mischievously.

"Hey, not so stormy, my Lord, you'll have plenty of opportunities to spank me on the bottom later on!" she kissed him passionately as a goodbye.

Then she ran to her black Camaro, which she had parked in the no-parking zone.

In the car, Lilly took her cell phone out of the glove compartment. "Time to call an old friend," she thought and dialled the number.

After it had rung about ten times, Hanna finally got in touch.

In a muffled voice, she asked, "Who is this?"

"It's me, Lilly!", she tried to come across as particularly flattering. At the other end of the line, a relieve was heard.

"My God! Thanks."

"Would you like to do something again sometime?"

Hanna replied only after some hesitation, "I don't know, I'm pretty tired."

"Oh, come on, make an effort, it'll be fun!"

Since Lilly did not stop harassing her, she reluctantly agreed.

Hanna couldn't suppress a certain annoyance.

"First, the stupid cow doesn't get in touch at all for weeks, and suddenly she wants to go out."

"I should best stay at home and leave her sitting," she murmured very quietly.

"Great, I'll meet you at the Chocolate Bar around 8:00?"

"Fine, whatever," the grim undertone was hard to miss this time; finally, she hung up.

In front of the bar, Lilly comfortably smoked a cigarette. Someone poked her from the right side. She winced, turned her head in that direction and saw her best friend.

"Do you have to sneak up on me like that?" She snorted in slight indignation.

"No, I don't have to, but you deserved a little punishment after your long absence!" Hanna replied amusedly.

"Okay, let's go inside," said Lilly.
Then they both went into the restaurant.

The Chocolate Bar was not only exceptional in its name; no, its name was simply the programme. Not only were there different cocktails or drinks with chocolate, but even beer. The food was refined with this sweet delicacy. Everything was offered for the heart of a chocolate addict. The two sat down at a table that was not directly near the window. When the waiter came after what felt like an eternity, Hanna chose a hot chocolate with whipped chocolate cream and a caramelised apple on a stick-on top. Lilly, however, decided to have a beer.

"How about we order the fondue", Lilly suggested.
"I already have the hot chocolate," Hanna said indecisively.
"Please!" Lilly looked at her, begging.
"All right, you talked me into it!"
Then they called the waitress again.
After a while, Hanna noticed how her bladder started to squeeze because she had taken a cocktail after the cocoa.
"You, I have to go to the toilet," she pushed the chair back to get up.
"It's about time," said Lilly. Then she made sure that Hanna was out of sight. There upon she pulled a small brown paper bag from her denim jacket to mix the contents called Amanita Muscaria, also called

toadstool, into Hanna's drink. The dose was, of course, not lethal; it was only meant to give the floozy an unforgettable trip plus a stay in the nuthouse. "Cheers!" Lilly stirred quickly. "Now you won't be able to cause us any more trouble," she said quietly. It didn't take long until Hanna came back from the toilet. She sat down on her chair and drank a gulp.

"The cocktail tastes kind of different."
"Does it?"
"Why would it taste different?"
"I don't know, but if I didn't know better, I'd say it tastes like mushrooms."
"No, it just seems that way!"
"Maybe," she said.

"Anyway, I think I'd better leave the rest."
"Your call!" Lilly looked at the clock, "It's late, I think it's time to go home."
"Oh yes, you're right; let's go," Hanna yawned exhaustedly, "I long for my bed."

Having arrived home, Hanna decided to watch some more TV. She held the remote control and thoughtlessly switched through all the channels. Suddenly she thought she could see a shadow out of the corner of her eye. She stood up jerkily and looked into the corner, but apart from the floral wallpaper, she could not see anything. She leaned back again to continue following the show. While she came to rest, she suddenly felt her hair was being pulled. At the same time, ice-cold hands

wrapped around her neck and
began to choke her. She gasped
and tried desperately with all
her strength to escape the
stranglehold. Hanna flailed
around violently with her arms
but still did not land a hit.
Then as abruptly as the attack
had begun, it was all over
again. After some time, Hanna
calmed down breathing.
She grabbed the baseball bat
and took up a combat-ready
stance. Every muscle in her
body was under extreme
tension, so that her phalanges
became visible under the skin.
There was absolute silence in
the apartment. She thought she
had only dreamed it all, but
suddenly a black figure
appeared right in front of her,
reaching up to the ceiling.
"Am I losing my mind or is this
really happening?" she asked

herself. It all seemed so surreal. Behind the figure, two more figures came out, which now grabbed her by the arms. She had no chance to free herself, no matter how much she resisted. Then she felt a sting that felt like a needle. Finally, Hanna sank into darkness.

Because of her hallucinations, she hadn't noticed how she had run out into the street. A neighbour who recognised her condition called the police.

No way out

When Hanna woke up, it took a few seconds before she could see clearly again. She tried to stand up but could not because her arms were tied to the bed. She looked around and found that she was lying in a hospital room. Next to her, a gaunt woman with unkempt black hair was snoring.

"How on earth did I get here?" She asked herself in wonder. Half an hour later a quite young nurse entered the room; she stepped towards Hanna and untied her restraints.

"Sorry, we had to restrain you because you were lashing out."

"What happened?" Hanna wanted to know.

"Afterwards you will be taken to the doctor, and then you can discuss everything with him," explained the nurse and left the room immediately.

Her bed neighbour seemed to have woken up by the conversation. She looked at Hanna. Her dark eyes had

collapsed and disappeared into
deep caves.
Then she started chattering
away.
"My name is Polly Gunter, I
already know your name, and
it's by the bed. I see they
freed you. I am here because
the voices in my head can't be
silent. So, it's not the first
time and what is about you?"
"One moment!" Hanna interrupted
her, "What hospital are we in
anyway?"
"At Mountclaire Mental
Hospital," Polly replied
calmly.
Only now did she realise that
the windows had bars.

"My name is Nurse Carla. I will
now take you to the doctor!"
An older sister with grey
streaks in her hair placed a
wheelchair in front of her.

"Would you please sit down?
It's a procedure while you're
under supervision."
Hanna sat in the thing without
enthusiasm. Then the nurse tied
a belt around her, which was
closed from behind.
"Is that really necessary?" she
asked shyly.
"As I mentioned before you are
under surveillance," the sister
said.
This was a clear indication
that no contradiction
whatsoever was tolerated.

The hallway of the clinic did
not make a particularly
inviting impression; it was
very gloomy, and the paint
splintered off the walls. As
they turned right towards the
elevator, two orderlies came
towards them, pushing a man in
front of them on a stretcher.

He looked lifeless; only his slightly rosy cheeks betrayed that this was not so. Hanna hastily averted her eyes from the scene.

In the elevator, the sister pressed the third button. When they reached the floor, they turned left and stopped in front of the fifth door.
Next to the door was a small sign saying, "Examination room 02."
Hanna was positioned in front of the examination table. After a few minutes, a doctor with short blond hair entered the treatment room.
He introduced himself "I am Dr. Alexander."
The nurse loosened the belt behind the wheelchair. Then Hanna sat down on the examination couch.

"Please remain seated upright," the doctor asked, shining a small lamp into her eyes. He also pulled a reflex hammer from one of the three drawers; then he tested her reflexes on her knees and feet. Next, the doctor asked her to touch her nose with her eyes closed. When the doctor had finished the physical examination, he sat down in front of the PC, typed something in and turned back to her

"I have to ask you now a few more questions."

"Okay," she replied.

"Are there any mental diseases in your family known?"

"No, not that I know of."

"Do you drink alcohol or use drugs?" The doctor smiled.

"Of course not!" Hanna sounded clearly outraged.

"Good, we are done here then,"
said Dr. Alexander
disinterested.
"By the way," he continued, "we
have already talked to Dr.
Klein on the phone and agreed
that it would not be wrong if
you stayed here for observation
for two weeks."

For Hanna, these words were a
punch in the gut. She had
firmly expected to be able to
go home immediately. Until now,
she didn't even know how she
had got here in the first place
"I wouldn't know what this was
n-necessary for, I am mentally
completely healthy!"
"Okay, but we still want to
make sure that there will be no
more problems."
"It's for your own good," the
doctor added and left the room.

For dinner, a bean stew was served, which bore a great resemblance to vomit.

"Oh, God, you want me to eat that?" Hanna wanted to throw up. However, for fear of attracting attention, she ate the plate empty. Her neighbour sat next to her and talked to herself the whole time. Hanna would have loved to shout at her for this and tell her to shut up. Only this would not have been a very good idea, so she pulled herself together. Even though she had only been here for a few hours, she was already able to experience what happened when you stepped out of line. Two orderlies were in the room with her, so it was not exceptionally difficult to feel like in jail. Shortly before, the two cops had also knocked down a man and moved

him to the isolation room where
he was just about to spend his
time.

After dinner, the lounge
opened. There was a large, flat
screen with various seating.
One of the caregivers switched
on the device. The series Love
and Passion was on, a soap
opera that Hanna couldn't get
much out of. However, it was
better to sit in front of the
TV than to spend all the time
in the room staring at the
wall. On the left side was a
billiard table, at which three
men played. Their names were
Martin, Andy and Tyler. Martin
constantly covered his face
with a cloth, but she noticed
that Andy was very cheeky. For
tomorrow, Brenda had announced
her visit, which gave her a
feeling of hope "Maybe I can

get out of here with her help,"
she hoped. "After all, I'm not
crazy!"

At the same time, Lilly was
sitting on the desk right in
front of him. Her legs were
crossed, she played around with
her toes on his tie, and then
they went down to his crotch.
Tom began to moan excitedly. He
pulled her to him and kissed
her. Meanwhile, his hand moved
under her blouse, gently
unfastening her bra. She laid
her head back, and then sat
down on his lap. Lilly felt his
penis getting hard.
"Thank God we got rid of them,"
she said, very relieved. She
gently kneaded his glans; he
moaned again.
"Yes", Tom replied and handed
her a portion of mushroom
powder, "But we're not done

yet, so do what I told you to do!"
He mentioned this in a very imperious way and with a violent push, he penetrated her longingly. Lilly emitted a soft, painfully distorted scream, and at the same time, the desire overwhelmed her. After they had slept together, she pushed her light brown dress down again and put the bag in her pocket.

Closed society

Brenda took a deep breath. Sunrays fell on the autumn leaves and made them shimmer golden. The two had decided to take a walk in the clinic park to get some fresh air.

Meanwhile, Hanna looked impassive. Brenda suspected that the medication was heavily sedating her. After a while, Hanna started talking

"You have to help me get out of here!" Brenda stopped and looked at her helplessly.
"How am I supposed to do that?" Hanna's expression became more alert, "Convince the doctors that I'm not crazy!"
"H-Help me to find the responsible for D-David's death so I can hunt him down!"
"Okay, just, how do I do this?"
"I don't know, just w-what do I do?"
"I'll see if I can make a difference, but I can't promise you anything!"

Brenda did not refuse her request because she had

received this recommendation from Dr. Alexander.

When Brenda left, Hanna retired to her room. Before that, however, she had to go to the medication dispensary. She never swallowed the pill but kept it in her cheek pocket until she could spit it into the toilet in the bathroom. Then she lay down in the rather hard bed, pulled the blanket over her head and turned on her side.

"Hope Brenda is successful," Hanna said a small emergency prayer before she fell asleep.

"Shut up," Martin said angrily, his blue eyes sparkled angrily.

"Why are you upset?" Dr. Miller asked.

"Because I'm tired of being provoked by him all the time."

"Why?" Andy replied, "You have a huge rhinoceros on your face too," he grinned, revealing his tooth gap.
Andy lost his left incisor at the age of eleven.
Neighbourhood children had thrown him into a pit for fun, where he stayed all night before he was rescued. Since then he suffered from claustrophobia.

Martin bashfully covered his nose again with the cloth. "Maybe Andy just wanted to encourage you to be a little more open and to think about your self-confidence, about your appearance," explained Dr. Miller. "Yes, maybe," Martin admitted crunchily.

For Hanna, the weekly group sessions were simply

ridiculous. The theatre took place about every two weeks. The initially promised two weeks for observation had in the meantime turned into six weeks. Since the doctors now assumed that she was schizophrenic, she could no longer hope to get out too soon. The hopelessness of her situation turned into an unspeakable desperation.

"Hanna, wouldn't you like to say something on the subject?" Dr. Miller addressed her.
Her thoughts startled her.
"Sorry, I wasn't paying attention just now."
"We were talking about what Martin could do to develop more self-confidence."
"Oh yes, yes, he could take off the scarf more often to face his fears."

"That's a fantastic idea!" Dr. Miller was thrilled.
"Very good Hanna!"

The psychologist praised her beyond all measure as if she had just proved the existence of God.
After the exuberant hymn of praise, Dr. Miller turned to the group again.

"One way to develop more self-confidence is to discover, among other things, who we ourselves are.
This concludes today's session, and I wish you all a pleasant day."
"Next week I will be giving other truisms of mine," Hanna mocked without saying it. She was glad that this nonsense was over now.

Brenda came home from shopping. She put the shopping bags down. Exhausted, she let herself fall into an armchair. Her feet burned like fire. Since she missed the bus and could not get a cab, she had to walk all the way.

"If only I had taken the car," she moaned. A week ago, she spoke with Dr. Alexander. Although he sounded very convincing, she still had doubts about the correctness of his assessment. Because Hanna had been completely healthy before her accident, went to work and led a normal life.

"So why should she suffer from schizophrenia now?" She thought that it was simply illogical. "Maybe the guilty person is actually trying to harm her. But how am I supposed to find him or her?" Brenda just did not know what to do. "Maybe I should talk to Tom about it again," she thought.

"Surprise!" Someone covered her eyes from behind. From the voice, however, Hanna immediately recognised that it could only be Lilly. She immediately turned to her; finally, they hugged each other.
"I never thought that you would come! " Hanna beamed full of joy.
"Why shouldn't I come to visit you, we are still friends after all, and today I found some time," Lilly replied casually.
"How are you doing?"

"Good, but I would feel even better if they dismissed me because I am absolutely fine!

I spoke to Brenda about this a few weeks ago and asked her to help me find the stalker. I would like to ask you the same; help me find the stalker."

Lilly was silent, in front of her stood a cup of coffee; of course, she had also brought Hanna one with a special ingredient. Then she asked "Are you really sure that the guilty party could be after you?"

"Yes!" Hanna explained seriously and began to cry. A tear dripped on the white table.

"Take a sip of coffee first, you'll feel better afterwards," Lilly said to her. Then she grabbed her hand and offered her a handkerchief, which she had previously taken out of her purse.

When Lilly left the clinic, she surprised herself at how smoothly everything had worked out. Nevertheless, she was even more amazed that it was so easy for her to keep her nerves. She felt a little sorry for Hanna. Only pity was not worth walking behind bars for a long time. What happened that evening had happened. This time she had decided to mix the powder with coffee, hoping the bitterness would mask the taste. On the whole, however, she did not care whether Hanna could taste the toadstool or not, because who would believe a crazy person.

A fog spread out before her eyes, Hanna could barely make out her bed neighbour, but at the same time, everything was

66

moving. Half an hour after Lilly's visit, she had difficulty maintaining her balance and was losing more and more of the orientation. "Should I call the nurse?" Polly asked irritated. Hanna would have loved to answer her; only her tongue was no longer able to form the words. She mumbled so much that no one could understand her. After what felt like an eternity, in which she wandered around helplessly, she took two arms again...

The next day, as when she was admitted, Hanna had to wait to be released from her restraints before she was allowed to get up. Her head felt like it was wrapped in absorbent cotton, and she had difficulty sitting quietly for long of time. In addition, as if that was not enough, Dr. Alexander told her during rounds that she would receive her medication by injection from now on. Polly had told them that she was worried and regularly disposed of the tablets in the toilet. The three of them pressed her on the bed, while the sister pricked her with the needle. Every contradiction was impossible. Hanna knew now that she could never escape.

An unusual friendship and resignation

"The picture looks great, Brenda," said Tom enthusiastically. Between Brenda and him, they developed a platonic but intimate friendship over the last weeks. It simply felt good to be able to talk about everything professionally, especially now, when Hanna was in such a bad condition. Her fears that there might be someone who wanted to harm her sister had, therefore, vanished into thin air. "Do you have a new car?" She had a hard time hiding her curiosity.

"No, I just took it to the garage to get it freshly painted."

"Do you like the new hue," Tom asked with not even feigned interest.

"Yes! It looks very elegant, really a very nice midnight blue!" Then she added "But we should get on with it now, otherwise we won't be finished."

"Of course, I didn't want to hold you up."

"I am very grateful to you for supporting us in this difficult time," said Brenda, visibly moved.

"Don't mention it and remember her condition will improve if she is properly medicated." Inwardly, Tom had to laugh at his own words and at his new friend who so willingly believed everything, he said.

"Hey, give me the remote control", Andy tore the remote control out of Martin's hand, "You've had it long enough now!"

"Hell, yeah, that's good!"

"You could have just told me that you wanted it!" Martin replied angrily.

"Do you two have to fight again?" Polly interfered. "You two idiots just can't get along!"

Hanna sat on the sofa and paid no attention to the discussion. Since she was under medication, nothing seemed really interest her. Meanwhile, while walking, she pulled her left leg because her muscles had become stiff. "Hanna! Time for lunch!" Polly shouted to her. After a while, she got up clumsily from the couch. As she had difficulty getting up, Polly offered her arm for support and pulled her up. In the dining room, Polly then lined up to serve the food for both of them. Two weeks ago, Hanna had another visit from her big sister. However, this no longer meant anything to her; she simply did not seem to care. A month ago, this would have been unthinkable, but Polly finally came back with the food and put one of the two trays in front of her.

"Today, we have something to eat," said Martin, who sat down next to the two women.

On the plate lay Spaghetti Bolognese with grated cheese. There was also a vanilla pudding with raspberry sauce for dessert.

"That's always like that on Sundays," Andy replied.

"For the rest of the week they serve us the usual dog chow." Hanna poked absently in her food.

"Don't you like it?" Polly asked anxiously.

"Hey, man, you can see they blew her brains out."

"In the upstairs closet... Lights out!"

"Enough, that's enough," Martin intervened clearly irritated.

"That you always have to say
things like that!"
"Sorry, I didn't mean it that
way," said Andy repentantly.
"It's okay," he said.

Hanna was unexpectedly to word.
Sometimes she could break
through her lethargy for a
short time. The fog in her head
then cleared for a brief
moment.

"That's going well," thought
Tom self-satisfied and unlocked
the door to his apartment.
Tom lived in a two-room
apartment in the most expensive
part of Hillbone. Whenever he
played the good friend for
Brenda, he felt a feeling of
absolute superiority. The need,
having power over others was
also one of the reasons why he
decided to become a

psychiatrist. Evan as a child
he was able to manipulate his
parents, teachers, and
classmates.
Other people had never had any
deep meaning for him; they
were nothing more than
characters in a play he was
staging. "Now it's just a
quick shower and then back to
the car and off to Lilly's,"
he was already ravenously
hungry.

Lilly got the
potato casserole from the oven
and had to take a hell of a lot
of care not to burn her
fingers. She quickly tipped the
dressing over the salad.
The doorbell rang to the minute
"Come in, the
Dinner is ready."
Tom took off his coat and took
off his shoes. He walked into

the living room and made himself comfortable on the couch. At the same time Lilly brought in the plates and cutlery
and set the table, she prepared the food on the plates. He tasted the casserole, and then he said, "A little too much salt, don't you think?" Of course, Tom knew that the casserole was not over-salted. However, he wanted to avoid that Lilly developed too much self-confidence, because this was the only way he could keep control over her.
In addition, this trick worked, instead of reacting hurt to the unjustified criticism, Lilly was simply disappointed in herself.

Meanwhile, Brenda lay at home in the bathtub, enjoying the warm water, listening to music and drinking a glass of red wine. Tomorrow she would go back to see Hanna. She hoped very much that she was feeling a little better by now. Even though Tom was able to calm her down, it was still a difficult sight to bear. After twenty minutes, she got out of the tub and wrapped herself in a big bath towel. She went to the bedroom put on her pyjamas and then went to the living room to read a little more. She finally fell asleep during a romance novel.

"Look what I brought you!" Brenda took a book with blank pages and a pencil from the bag next to her and handed them both over to Hanna.

"I think it might help you if you wrote down what you do or what goes through your mind all day," she explained.

"I don't know," Hanna replied. Except for this one sentence, she had not yet contributed anything to the conversation. The woman sitting in front of Brenda had nothing to do with the person she had once grown up with the changes were frightening.

"Shall we go for a walk?" Brenda made the suggestion. Without showing the slightest emotion, Hanna stood up, grabbed the walker she had been given a week before and limped into the clinic park with Brenda.

When Brenda was back home, she picked up the phone to call Tom, but only the answering machine answered. Therefore, she left him a message asking him to call back as soon as possible. Despite all his explanations, Hanna's condition worried her more and more.

Annoyed, he looked at his cell phone.
"Not this one again!" Tom would have loved to throw the phone against the wall.
"Hello, Brenda, great you called. Any news?"
"No, Hanna is still not getting better, and I even have the impression that it got worse," she started sobbing. "Tom, she needs a walker now, although she could walk perfectly normal!"
"I see, what do you say we meet at your studio around 7:45 p.m.?"

Brenda was anything but thrilled about having to go to the studio again tonight, so she made the counterproposal that he come to her. Since Tom wanted to get the matter out of the way as quickly as possible, he agreed without objection. Finally, he had a lot of fun to fool this bitch. Tonight, however, he would have preferred to go to squash with a friend of his. "The movement disorders are clearly a result of the medication." He knew it could happen, especially when it was administered to a person who did not need it at all.

Hanna's world

She held the pencil convulsively in her right hand. The letters that Hanna brought to paper were spidery, which was due to the constant slight trembling of her hand. Nevertheless, she was feeling better than the weeks before because the doctors had reduced the dose a little.

She wrote. "The day before yesterday, the neighbour from the opposite room, Rick Thomas, was found hanged in the shower.

Sister Belinda, a still very young nurse whose shrill scream could heard throughout the building after she discovered his body hanging rigidly down found him. Andy has been busy ever since, bragging everywhere that he caught a glimpse of the dead man for a split second.

He said, 'His eyes were twisted so that only the white was visible, and the tongue was hanging out of his mouth!' What a show-off."

Hanna put down the pencil, her
hand began to tremble more, and
the writing became illegible.

The next day she wrote in her
Diary. "We all knocked at the
rhythm onto our drums, and we went
in circles until Mrs Lipinsky called
'Stop'. The music and dance therapy
are the only good in this dump,
although the chick who teaches it
seems to be crazy herself. Mrs
Lipinsky is a redheaded snipe whose
hairstyle looks like she's hiding a bird's
nest in it..."

"Hello trembler, are you
coming?" Andy had sneaked up on
her from behind. Hanna reacted
angrily and hissed at him
bitchily

"Can't you knock, and besides, my name is not trembler!" Andy blushed

"Sorry, I didn't mean to hurt you!"

"You know, words often leave my mouth before I realise what I said."

She sighed, and then replied...

"It's okay; I know you can't always control yourself."

He turned around and went for the door, and just before Andy stopped, "Are you gone play bingo or not?"

"Of course!", ever since she was better, Hanna was happy for every change.

At bingo there was, of course, no money to win. Instead, one was allowed win smaller material prizes such as funny pens or baskets, which were filled with cosmetics. And whoever hit the jackpot was allowed to determine what was watched on television for that week. The only restriction was that pornography was completely prohibited. Andy was very much hoping to win the grand prize this week.

The next morning Martin, Andy and Polly were still discussing yesterday's bingo game. While Hanna abstained from the discussion.

"Too bad," whined Andy, "Star Wars is on Tuesday on TV. I can forget about that movie now!" "Oh, we were really lucky," commented Martin spiteful. "Stop it!" Polly shook her head uncomprehendingly.

"Why? I am not willing to look at that nonsense!"

"Still, you could go more toward him," the bipolar Tyler Watkins interfered surprisingly.

"Approach him more," Martin followed him.

"He must first show me that he can keep his fucking mouth shut!"

"What have you got against Andy?" Tyler asked further.

"Oh, it just gets on my nerves that he always teases me about my nose."

"I'm not teasing you about your nose, I'm teasing you about the face cloth," Andy justified his teasing; "I bet you can't leave that thing off for a week."

"And I bet you're wrong!" Martin countered.

Because the doctors trusted her now, Hanna was given pills again, which she could take in the toilet or the bathroom as usual.

In the trash can of the clinic park. Only this time she was even more careful not to be caught doing it again. She had been clean for a week, and with each day that her brain was no longer flooded with drugs, she was able to think more clearly. Her shaking had also subsided considerably in the meantime, but she continued to fake it in order not to arouse suspicion. 9:30 a.m., in five minutes, the next group session took place. Unlike before, she found it very exciting to observe the development of the others. Martin, for example, now took off his face cloth during dinner, something that had been unimaginable until recently.

In the group room, they set up the chairs in a circle and waited for Dr. Miller to open the session.

"I hear you won the bet; I am proud of you, Martin," praised Dr Miller.

The therapist looked at him with great satisfaction.

"Yes," he replied, "But I would never have given Andy the triumph!"

"Still, I cover my nose again as of today!"

"You betcha. Rudi trunk!" Andy grunted like a pig. Hanna could not stop giggling.

"Well then, let's continue."

"Hanna, is there something you want to discuss with us today?"

"No, I have nothing I want to talk about."

"Are you sure? After all, you've suffered a terrible loss, haven't you?"
"Yes, but I don't want to talk about it in this circle."
"So... good", Dr. Miller accepted grudgingly Hanna's decision.
Finally, he gave Martin his attention again "Martin, don't you want to tell us how you felt when you first took off the scarf?"
"Mmm, how can I best describe it?"
"First of all, I felt naked, and I thought about how others would react to my appearance."
"What were your worst fears?"
"That I'll be laughed at."
"Why should we laugh at you?"
"Because I'm ugly."
"And have your expectations of being laughed at materialised

because of your appearance?"

"Fortunately, no."

"Now that your fears are unfounded, what's preventing you from leaving the cloth off permanently?"

"The feeling of being disfigured and unattractive."

"I don't know. I can't explain it rationally."

Martin didn't say how his mother had ridiculed him as a child because of his nose. She regularly compared it to that of his father, who left the family when Martin was five years old. His mother always used to say, "You have exactly the same pig's nose like your father!"

"Does anyone want to say anything about Martin's problem?" Dr. Miller glanced questioningly into the round.

After a few minutes, Tyler Watkins spoke up

"Martin looks perfectly normal; the rag on his face is silly."

"Thank you, Tyler, for your point of view."

"Anyone else who has anything to say on the subject?"

"Or who has a topic of their own that they would like to discuss," Dr. Miller looked around and waited a few seconds.

"All right, if no one else has anything to discuss, I'd say we'll end the session for today, and I wish you all a very good day."

Andy ran after him, tapped him on the shoulder and finally said, "Well done, buddy; I never thought you could get over it!"

Shocked!

Brenda cleared the table. Tom
and Lilly had left the door
just before. She was glad that
he arranged that Hanna didn't
get any more injections. In the
meantime, on his advice, she
had taken legal care of Hanna.
At first, she did not like the
idea at all because she did not
want to restrict her sister's
basic rights without
justification. However, the
idea of not being able to help
her properly otherwise robbed
her of even more sleep. So, she
had agreed. Lilly had also
promised to visit Hanna
tomorrow.

Lilly walked together with
Hanna into the visitor's room.
Last night she had also

received further instructions
from Tom after they had been
with Brenda. As usual, she
brought two cups of coffee.
"How are you today?"
She asked with interest and put
one of the cups down in front
of Hanna.
"I feel a little better."
"Well, happy for you."
"Are you still enjoying your
work?"
"Absolutely, everything is
fine, just a lot to do."
"You have no idea how much I
envy you!"
"I'm so fucking sick of being
cooped up in this cuckoo's
nest."
Lilly looked at her with sad
eyes. Finally, she replied,
"You have to think about what
this could bring you."
"Are you serious? What s-should
it get me? They're just

treating me like a madwoman," Hanna replied angrily, then excused herself from running out onto the balcony.

When she was gone, Lilly noticed that the mushroom powder was still in her bag. She hurriedly took it out and emptied it into the cup.

"What are you doing, please?" Lilly hadn't noticed that Hanna had come back. She winced in shock "I, uh, just put sugar in your coffee, that's all."

"Sugar?"

"You remember that I drink coffee without sugar, right?"

"Really?"

"Sorry, I completely forgot." Hanna sipped the coffee, and this time she could clearly taste the mushrooms. She looked at her friend seriously; then she asked Lilly again to tell her what she had put in her coffee. Nevertheless, Lilly remained silent. Instead, she ran head over heels out of the clinic without saying a word.

"Damn it, damn it, damn it!" "The bitch caught me!" Lilly sat down behind the steering wheel. She took her smartphone and sent Tom a text with the message. "SOS!"

At that moment, Tom was busy writing a report for a judge friend of his. At that moment, his cell phone rang, which didn't please him very much. Everyone who knew him knew very well how much he detested being disturbed at work. Therefore, he hoped very much for the one who dared to do so anyway that there was an important reason for it. After a cursory glance at the display, he again turned, unmoved, to the expert opinion.

At home, "You stupid turkey! "Shouted Tom at Lilly.
"Can't you do anything right?" He paused several times deeply so as not to lose his temper.
"I didn't mean to," she replied in a tearful voice, "I just forgot!"
"Forgot!" He said contemptuously.
"Anyway, I will have to call the clinic now."
"Perhaps I can still limit the damage you have done in your thoughtlessness! You are suffering from idiocy, unbelievable!"

Dr. Andre Alexander was a little astonished at what his colleague had just reported to him. With Miss Mooreland, he was still never reported aggressive behaviour by the nursing staff. However, well, there was always the first time, probably the medicine was not sufficient yet, which made other measures necessary.

"That word does not exist," protested Martin as Andy tried to place the word tailhound. Martin, Andy, Polly, Hanna and Tyler were playing Scrabble. Andy was cheating for the third time, which Tyler enjoyed very much.
It was Hanna's turn when two male nurses surprisingly came in, grabbed her by the arms and took her away. They led her into a room where there was a couch with buckles. Hanna was asked to lie down on the couch, after which her arms and legs were fixed. Afterwards, a bite

splint was put in her mouth.
Finally, the doctor looked for
a vein to give her a milky
looking liquid. Fortunately,
thanks to the anaesthesia, she
did not notice the subsequent
electric shock, which triggered
a seizure.

While she regained
consciousness, Hanna felt a
strong head - and
jaw pains. Everything seemed
strange all of a sudden; even
Polly did not recognise her at
first sight. Something had
pressed the reset button in her
head, she felt. Only what had
happened? She held her head.
Her skull was humming like
after a night of drinking.
Hanna had the impression that
her brain was about to explode.
"Fucking feeling what? But the
pain will subside in a few

hours," Polly told her
confidently. "You can prepare
yourself to be grilled every
two or three days from now on."
"What do you mean by that?"
Polly rolled her eyes "That
they put 200 volts through your
brain.
That's what I'm trying to say."
She looked at Polly in horror.
"You're kidding!"
"No, why?"
"For heaven's sake," Hanna
whimpered full of horror.
Five minutes later, sister
Carla entered the room and
brought her a tablet against
the pain.
"Do you have to urinate?" she
asked icily.
Hanna actually felt the need to
pee "Yes, why?"
"Because then I have to support
you."

As soon as she got up, she understood what the nurse meant. Her legs suddenly seemed to be made of rubber, and she could hardly stand on them.

"Are you sure it's safe?" Brenda didn't have a good feeling about it, and she was used to trusting it.
"For sure. The electroshock therapy is an old and well-proven procedure," Tom explained holding his teacup again.
"I am well aware that it sounds brutal to you, but this treatment method is excellent for getting a brain that has gone out of sync back into order."
"Oh, before I forget, please don't be surprised if Hanna tells you that Lilly put something in her coffee. At

least she's still pretty
paranoid."
"Understood," Brenda replied
but did not seem completely
convinced.

The electric shocks impacted
Hanna significantly more than
the drugs before. After each
treatment, it took longer for
her memory to return. Her life,
if you could still call it
that, had now finally become
hell on earth. In order to
bring her memory back, she
always noted down immediately
what she could remember or what
she did. In this way, she
managed not to lose the red
thread. However, Lilly's visit
was literally erased from her
memory. Only her subconscious
signalled to her that there was
something she absolutely had to
remember.

Lilly was plagued by remorse. Actually, she only wanted to get Hanna out of the way, not destroy her, but that's exactly what she helped to do. Tom had informed her that permanent damage from the treatment was within the realm of probability. Could she really be responsible for that? And was he even worth it to take part in this scheming and dangerous game? After all, he caused the accident and not her. If she had filed a report at the time, she might not have been prosecuted under criminal law. Now she was in too deep to go back. Tom always knew how to push the right buttons on her, that God damned son of a bitch. Then she drank another glass of wine until she emptied the bottle.

In the land of nightmares

Hanna ran through the forest like a chased deer. A person who hid the face behind a mask followed her. After a few meters, the thicket finally cleared, and a cottage appeared in the distance. She hurriedly ran towards it. Shortly after she reached the door, she tried to open it, but the knob was so rusty that it did not move a millimetre. Desperately she searched for another entrance, but the windows were also barricaded. Suddenly she heard footsteps coming closer and closer. Without turning around,

she knew that it was her
pursuer.

Hanna woke up with a beating
heart. Dazed, she looked for
the light switch of the bedside
lamp. In the glow of the light,
the tension gradually began to
ease from her. Next to her,
Polly was sleeping peacefully.
She took the diary and the
pencil and briefly noted down
the dream. From various books,
that Dr. Klein had recommended
to her; she knew that dreams
contained messages from the
subconscious. Perhaps the dream
was the key to her remembering.

"Too bad Tyler isn't here now."
Andy was sitting on the park
bench with Polly.
"You got that right, though,
Andy," Polly agreed, flicking
his wrist. Recently, she

clicked her tongue more strongly. Polly was first admitted to psychiatry at the age of twenty when she was studying biology. At the time, she had gotten so involved in her studies that one day she collapsed. Polly slept and ate very little. At some point, she developed the delusional idea that the university everywhere had planted bugs to spy on her. After her first hospital stay, Polly recovered relatively well, but then she stopped taking her pills on her own, which led to a relapse, which was followed by the next one. Similarly, Tyler unexpectedly slipped into a depressive phase again last week. In order to prevent a suicide like Rick Thomas', the clinic immediately transferred him to the closed ward. There he was monitored

for twenty-four hours. Neither
Andy, Polly nor Martin envied
him because accommodation in
the closed ward usually meant
spending the whole day alone in
a room with a window. Often, he
was also tied to the bed and
waited for time to pass. In
principle, just the right thing
to make an already depressed
person even more depressed.
That is why they called this
department the Psycho Prison.

Tonight, Hanna wanted to unmask
her persecutor at least that
was what she had firmly in
mind. To achieve this goal, she
visualised the scene in which
she asked the persecutor to
take off mask before falling
asleep until her eyes closed.

"Would you like some more wine,
Tom?"

"I'd love some," he held his glass out to Brenda.

2I don't have to drive today, right, Lilly?" Tom looked at her friendly but determined.

"Did I ever tell you that I've had the same dream since I was five years old?" Brenda dunked a piece of bread in the cheese.

"No! Sounds very interesting though, do you want to talk to us about it?" Brenda hesitated "I don't know; it's a really stupid dream."

"We love silly dreams", he leaned back comfortably and sipped on his wine glass. "All right. The dream always begins with me standing alone in a meadow. Afterwards, I always find myself on the shore of a lake. From which, after a while, a monster emerges and invites me to go with him."

"Does this monster, by any chance, resemble Nessie?" Lilly joked.

"Are you afraid of the monster, or are you sympathetic to it?" Tom followed up. "No, I'm not afraid of it, and it looks more like a dragon," she cleared her throat. "I'm always disappointed in the dreams where I can't go with him."

"Well, if we apply Freud's thesis, the lake would stand for the uterus and the dragon for the penis, so your dream is an expression of penis envy."

"C.G. Jung, on the other hand, would ask you what the dream means to yourself," Tom explained.

"I don't know what it means to me, but I think the penis theory is bullshit."

"Since I have the dream mainly in stressful situations, I think it is an expression of overload."

"That's very likely," he agreed with her resolutely. "By the way, I think it's great that you've cleared away all the boxes in the meantime."

"Yes, I was finally able to pull myself together to unpack. I'm now in my new life."

"John is now definitely a thing of the past!"

"I am happy for you," Tom replied.

"Well," Brenda said, and then she raised her glass, "Let's drink to the future!"

"What an entertaining evening, don't you think?" Lilly drove the car and kept quiet. Then she replied, "You have to suck up to her all the

time, you do enough to them
anyway!
"Oh, is someone jealous?"
"No, I'm not!"
"Then what's your problem?"
"Don't play dumb!"
"It's about you letting Brenda
believe that Hanna is insane,
and then lock her up in a psych
ward because you killed the
love of her life consciously!"
"The accident was not
intentional!"
"Besides, you're not one
hundred per cent innocent of
it!" He clenched his hands to
fists.
"Yes, but after that, you
shirked your responsibilities!"
"And who helped me get away
with it?"
"I only did what you forced me
to do!" She could hardly hide
her anger.

"Pull over," he ordered her
harshly.
"Why? We're in the middle of
nowhere!"
When he understood that Lilly
would not obey him this time,
Tom grabbed the steering wheel
and steered his Ford right into
a forest path. Lilly could just
brake.
"Are you crazy? Are you trying
to kill us both?" Tom got out
without a word, walked around
the car, opened the driver's
door and turned the
car keys.
"Get out," he growled
threateningly.
"You can kiss my ass," she
began to look excitedly in her
handbag for a taser.
"So, I should kiss your ass?
I'll show you where I'm going
to lick you," he grabbed her
brutally by the hair and

dragged her out of the vehicle.
"Stop it! You're hurting me",
Lilly tried desperately to give
him a strong kick in the balls,
but Tom was physically superior
to her.
He dragged her behind the
bushes, threw her roughly to
the ground, pushed up her skirt
and tore her lace underwear off
the body.
"Now I'm going to teach you
a lesson!"
He brutally penetrated her
rectum, so that she felt
pain curved.
"Well, how do you like that?"
he gasped scornfully.
Tom ignored Lilly's cries as
well as her plead for mercy,
her suffering even increased
his desire, and while he came,
he had the feeling that a
volcano erupted from his dick.
After raping her, he calmly

pulled up his jeans and walked
calmly to the car to leave her
in the undergrowth to herself.
It took Lilly sometime before
the shock subsided. She freed
her mouth from the leaves she
had almost choked on and
arranged her clothes.
proximity. Since she had heard
the Ford driving away, she knew
that he was no longer in the
vicinity. Lilly wandered a long
the road in the hope that
somebody would stop.
After a few meters or miles,
she was fortunately picked up
by a group of young people who
were on their way home from a
party.

Back home, Lilly could hardly
wait to get in the shower.
There she noticed that her anus
was bleeding slightly. For a
split second, she thought about

going to the emergency room, but she would certainly have had many unpleasant questions asked, so she decided against it. She turned on the water and soaped herself thoroughly, but as much as Lilly washed herself, the inner dirt stuck to her like bad luck.

In the meantime, Hanna had dreamed that she had arrived at the hut. Behind her, she heard the steps again, but instead of panicking, she stood still. She let the masked man come closer until he stopped right in front of her. Courageously, she stepped closer to the stranger, and then she asked, "Who are you?"
Slowly the stranger raised his hands towards her face; he pulled off the mask and out came... her best friend!

Insights and confessions

The next morning Hanna stared at the name she had written down and tried to make sense of it. "Why did Lilly appear to me in a dream?" She asked herself. Hanna hoped very much that she would soon find an answer to it.

Lilly looked in the mirror the day after. A large bruise had become visible on her left cheek. She took the camouflage makeup out of the cupboard and gently dabbed the injury with it. It was not the first time that she had to conceal wounds, firstly because Tom often slipped his hand when he was in a bad mood, and secondly

because her father beat her
when she was still a child.
Outbreaks of violence were the
agenda in her childhood,
because her father regularly
beat up Lilly and her mother
when he drank too much. To
protect herself, Lilly would
lock herself in her room
whenever she heard that her
father came from the pub drunk.
It was not unusual for him to
step violently into the door
with all his rage such that
Lilly feared she would burst at
any moment.

After the violence, Tom thought
about bringing her some flowers
tonight. "As a little
compensation, so to speak,
since I was pretty hard on her
yesterday," he smiled at the
thought. At the same time, Tom

felt himself getting stiff again.

"Are you still thinking about your dream?" Polly had just returned from the gym, where she had played table tennis with Tyler, who was feeling better.
"Yeah, it just doesn't leave me."
"I think I know why Lilly appeared to you." Hanna sat up excitedly "Let's hear!"
"She visit you a few weeks ago, but you have forgotten. I suppose the dream is to remind you of that very fact."
"As I recall, you were quite upset after her visit."
Suddenly the scales fell from Hanna's eyes. She remembered again that she had caught her best friend, mixing a mysterious powder into her

coffee. There was only one way to get to the bottom of this. She had to notify Brenda and convince her to help her confront Lilly.

"I am so tired of being nothing more than an attractive toy for this egomaniac," murmured Lilly while cleaning the glass table. Tom had left her a message on the answering machine that he will come over tonight and that she should cook for him. There was not a word of regret. However, from experience, she knew that this would not fail to happen. Surely, he came again with flowers from Chips' 99 Cent gas station, which you could throw in the trash after one day. Lilly had tried several times to leave the prison of emotional dependence, but each time she had failed miserably. Too much of the learned behaviour patterns were burned into her soul because love meant violence for her. Finally, he rang the doorbell.

What Hanna had just told her on the phone was crazy, Brenda believed. Why would Lilly want to poison her? On Thursday, Brenda promised her she would come by with Lilly. Then Hanna could personally convince herself that her suspicions were completely out of the air. Apparently, she was still not feeling any better. Hanna had asked her to bring drinks to the visit to lure Lilly into the trap. For Brenda, the accusations were simply groundless.

"That smells good!" Tom bit into the burger with a big appetite. Lilly had two burgers taken out of the freezer. Actually, he did not like convenience food, as he put it, but she knew how to prepare it so that he no longer tasted the difference. She served the burger with fried mushrooms and onions, accompanied by a homemade honey-mustard sauce.

"By the way, I have something else for you here," Tom pushed a bag of mushroom powder over to her again.

"You know I don't want to do that anymore!"

"There's no turning back now!"

"To stop now would mean that it was all for nothing and Hanna's memory is coming back."

Lilly moaned exhausted, when

looking at her face, it showed clearly that she had enough of the whole shit.

"All right," she said and accepted the brown thing with disgust.

When she had pulled the ticket, Brenda drove to the parking garage.

"We're here," she said to Lilly.

Together they stepped out of the lift.

"I am curious how Hanna is doing today," Lilly said thoughtfully.

Her hands were wet, and she had a lump in her throat. "Oh, how should she react?"

"She will be happy to see you," Brenda replied confidently.

Then they passed the entrance.

In the visitor's room, Hanna was already waiting for them; Lilly avoided any eye contact with her. Brenda placed the three cups on the table; she had taken tea instead of coffee for herself.

"Well, how are you," Brenda began the conversation as casually as possible.

"Shitty as usual." Hanna kept looking over at Lilly, and her friend kept staring at the floor. "What have you been up to today," Brenda continued. "Nothing, what can you do here except eat, sleep and watch TV." "But no, wait; this morning we had art therapy."

"So, you did something, after all."

"Fine," said Brenda.

Hanna felt a need after a while, and Brenda too. But instead of going to the toilet,

they both ran outside and hid
behind the wall so they could
still see Lilly.
"Now you will see for yourself
that your accusations are
unfounded," Brenda said.
"Wait and see, maybe you will
be the surprised one!" They
looked over at Lilly
expectantly. Nothing happened
for a long time, but suddenly
they saw Lilly take a small
brown package out of her purse
and empty the contents into
Hanna's coffee. Brenda was
shocked, "Stop it immediately,"
she explained curtly.
Lilly was terrified and dropped
the brown package, scattering
the powder all over the table.

"What did you put Hanna in the
coffee?"
"Nothing, just sugar," she
replied helplessly.

"Don't call us stupid," Brenda said furiously. "Since when is sugar sold in little brown bags?"

Lilly was desperately looking for an explanation, but she just couldn't find one, at some point the pressure became too much and she understood that the game was over now. After a brief confession, she then willingly let Brenda take her to the nearest police station.

Epilogue

Warm sunrays fell on her face. Hanna was happier than she had been for a long time. Even if no punishment in the world could bring David back to life, it was still a good feeling to know how the accident happened.

And above all to know that, she had never been mentally ill. Lilly accepted to be detained because of her willingness to cooperate with the police, with a suspended sentence of which she also decided to start psychotherapy in order to work through their negative childhood experiences. Dr. Tom Klein, on the other hand, was punished and sentenced to ten years in prison.

He was able to be discharged with good conduct at the earliest in eight years. His license as a doctor had also been revoked.

"Who knows, maybe one day he will fry burgers and fries," thought Hanna. She smiled broadly, and then closed the front door behind her, because her new friends Polly, Andy,

Martin and Tyler were already
waiting for her.

The End

Herstellung und Verlag:
BoD - Books on Demand, Norderstedt
ISBN 978-3-7526-2525-7